DO NOT OPEN

DO NOT OPEN

by Brinton Turkle

A PUFFIN UNICORN

Miss Moody lived at land's end with Captain Kidd. Captain Kidd wasn't the famous pirate; he was a cat. One morning after a storm, Miss Moody found him washed up on the beach. He was nearly drowned. She nursed him until he was well, and he repaid her kindness by keeping her cottage free of mice.

Captain Kidd hated storms. Miss Moody loved them. Just about everything in her cottage was found on the beach after a storm, even the handsome banjo clock over her fireplace. The only thing wrong with it was, it wouldn't go. The hands always pointed to twenty minutes to four o'clock.

Late one September afternoon, the sky
darkened. Wind blustered up from the
southeast. Miss Moody knew what was
coming. She shut the windows and lit a
cheery fire in the fireplace. Then she made
a delicious chowder for supper. There was

enough for Captain Kidd, but he wouldn't come out from under her bed to eat it.

Lightning flashed. Thunder crashed. Rain dashed against the windows. All evening the wind howled furiously and tried to blow the little cottage to Halifax.

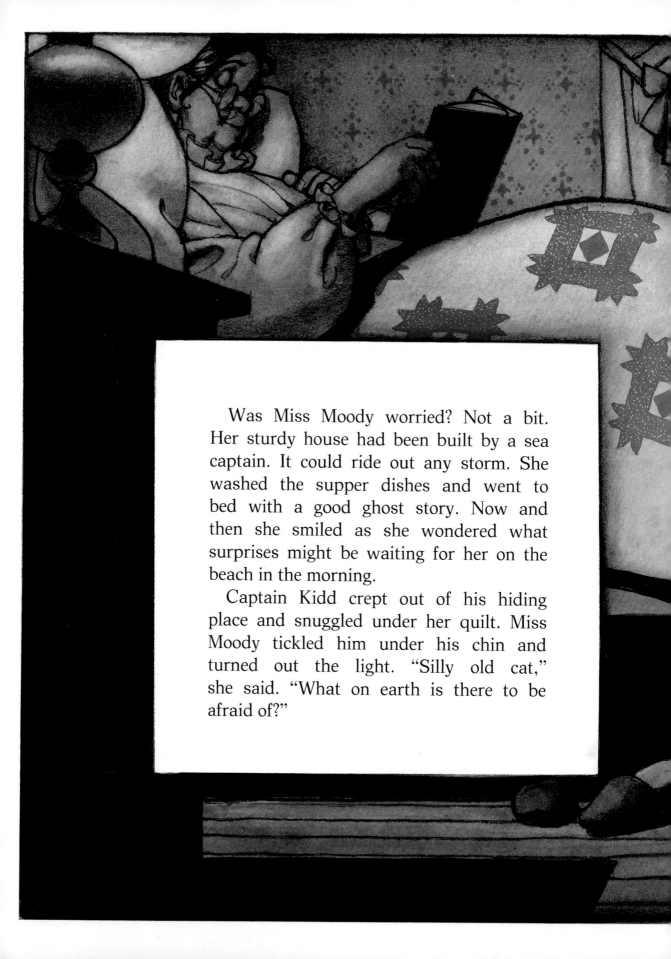

Was Miss Moody worried? Not a bit. Her sturdy house had been built by a sea captain. It could ride out any storm. She washed the supper dishes and went to bed with a good ghost story. Now and then she smiled as she wondered what surprises might be waiting for her on the beach in the morning.

Captain Kidd crept out of his hiding place and snuggled under her quilt. Miss Moody tickled him under his chin and turned out the light. "Silly old cat," she said. "What on earth is there to be afraid of?"

After a quick breakfast the next morning, Miss Moody got out the old wheelbarrow. She and Captain Kidd were ready for the treasure hunt.

The first thing she found was a pretty tin box full of wet cookies. Just what she needed for her postcard collection. She dumped out the cookies and stowed the box in her wheelbarrow.

Then she saw something red in the sand. It was a rug. She shook it out. One corner was missing, but it would look just lovely in her bedroom. The torn end could be tucked under the chest of drawers. She stowed the rug in her wheelbarrow.

She next came upon a pile of driftwood.
What gorgeous colors it would make burn-
ing in her fireplace! There was too much
for one load, so she stowed as much as
she could in her wheelbarrow and headed
home. She would come back for the rest
later.

Captain Kidd saw it first and he didn't like it at all. Nearly hidden in the sand was a small dark bottle. Colored bottles of all kinds hung in Miss Moody's west window. When the sun shone through them, it was like being in church. But there were no deep purple bottles like this one. It was closed tight. These words were scratched on it: DO NOT OPEN.

A voice said, "What do you want more than anything in the world?"

More than anything in the world, Miss Moody wanted her banjo clock to run properly: to tick and bong like banjo clocks are supposed to do. But she was certainly not about to tell this to a stranger. "None of your beeswax!" she snapped and turned around to see who had sneaked up behind her.

No one was anywhere in sight. She couldn't even see Captain Kidd for a moment. Then she noticed his tail twitching from under the wheelbarrow.

"I'll give you whatever you want if you'll just let me out. Pretty please?"

The voice was coming from the bottle! Miss Moody almost dropped it. "Who *are* you?" she gasped.

"I'm a poor little child. I was put in here by a wicked magician. I want to go home to my mama. Pull out the stopper. Please free me!"

Should she open the bottle?

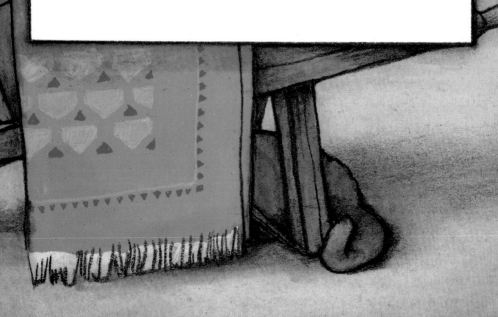

Miss Moody could not stand hearing a child cry. She tugged at the stopper. Suddenly it popped out.

Smoke trickled out of the bottle. She threw it on the sand. The smoke came out in billows, twisting into a big black cloud. The bottle burst. From inside the cloud came horrid laughter. It was not the laughter of a child.

"FREE!" roared a voice like thunder.

The smoke cleared away and Miss Moody was staring at the biggest, ugliest creature she had ever seen.

"Thank you, madam," it said. "Too bad you didn't make a wish. You could have had anything you wanted—gold, jewels, a palace. I could have made you a queen or a president. Now I must get to work."

"Work?" said the astonished Miss Moody.

"Lots of work. When anyone wants to steal or cheat or lie or hurt someone else or start a nice little war, I help them do it." The creature laughed. "Just for fun, I get into people's dreams. Children wake up screaming."

"That's just what you are," said Miss
Moody. "A bad, bad dream."

"Why aren't you afraid of me?"

"Because I'm not afraid of anything I
don't believe in. And I don't believe in
you for a minute."

The creature grew bigger and uglier.
"Now are you afraid of me?" it said.

"No," said Miss Moody.

The creature grew even bigger and even uglier. "Are you still not afraid of me?" it snarled.

"Getting bigger and uglier doesn't scare me," said Miss Moody. "I'm only afraid of mice. And you can't grow small like a little mouse."

The creature vanished.

At Miss Moody's feet was a tiny gray mouse.

Captain Kidd pounced. So quickly it didn't have time to squeak, he killed and swallowed the mouse.

"Captain!" cried Miss Moody. "Are you all right?"

Captain Kidd burped.

Miss Moody, Captain Kidd and the wheelbarrow all went home, wobbling a little bit.

Before they got to the cottage, Miss Moody heard it: "Bong! Bong! Bong! Bong! Bong! Bong! Bong! Bong!" She rushed inside.

The handsome banjo clock over the fireplace was ticking away busily. And the hands pointed to one minute past eight o'clock.